# The
# Gift

Written by
## Kathy Chase Young
Illustrated by
## Pamela P. Finch

Tishomingo Tree Press, Hattiesburg Mississippi

Published by:
Tishomingo Tree Press
606 Bay Street
Hattiesburg Mississippi 39401
www.tishomingotree.com

ISBN: 0-9768861-0-3

Printed in The Untied States of America

10 9 8 7 6 5 4 3 2

In memory of my mother
Betty Chandler,
who was a gift to so many.

-KCY

Dedicated to my sweet family-
Marc, Allison, Caitlin and Molly Grace.

-PF

A pleasant breeze stirred the warmth in the cozy kitchen on the bright October afternoon. The Saturday chores had been completed and the boys were out of the house until suppertime. It was a rare quiet moment in the usually busy home. Janie had been waiting all day for this precious time with her mother. She had run back and forth from the kitchen between each task hoping for a chance to help her mama make the family's favorite chocolate cake.

"Come on, I don't want you to miss out," Mama had called as she took the pans from the cabinet. Little feet had scooted across the tile floor and tippy toes had helped to reach the soap and water at the kitchen faucet. It was time! On the counter Janie sat licking the last bit of chocolate off of a smooth shiny beater.

"Mama, your cake is the best cake in the whole wide world." Her mama smiled. She thought so too. It had been her favorite since she was a girl.

"Mama, when I get big, will you give me the recipe?" asked Janie.

"Goodness yes, you know I will," her mother replied. "When Mama, when?" Janie asked again.

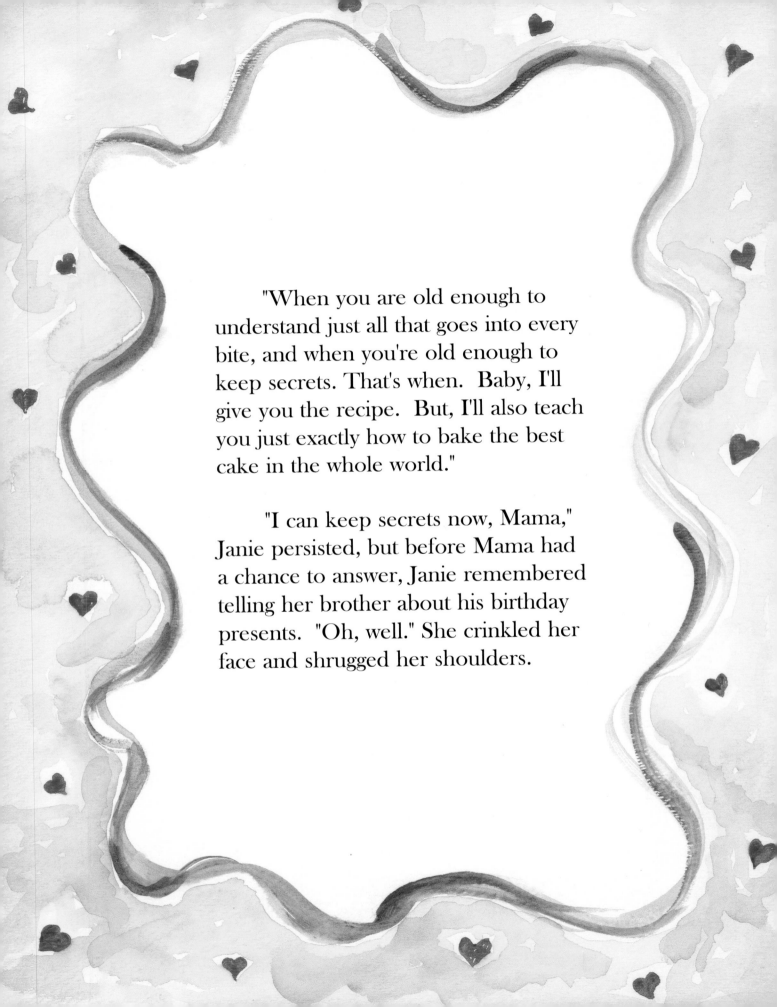

"When you are old enough to understand just all that goes into every bite, and when you're old enough to keep secrets. That's when.  Baby, I'll give you the recipe.  But, I'll also teach you just exactly how to bake the best cake in the whole world."

"I can keep secrets now, Mama," Janie persisted, but before Mama had a chance to answer, Janie remembered telling her brother about his birthday presents.  "Oh, well." She crinkled her face and shrugged her shoulders.

Janie's mama tickled her a little on the neck as she reached over to take the big spoon from the drawer. Janie continued her questions. "Mama, why do you keep that recipe so secret? You're always telling me that I should share with other folks. Last week, you made me share my bike with Billy. You won't even share it with Mrs. Laura and she's your best friend!"

"Well," her mother answered, "that's how special things stay special. There are a few things that you've got to keep all to yourself and guard them closely, you hear?"

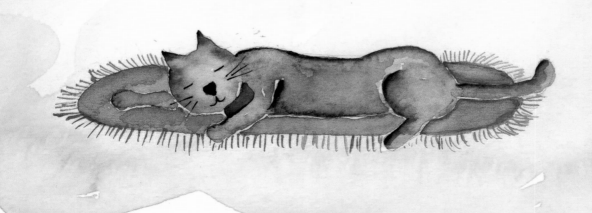

Mother continued, "Janie, do you remember how my mother used to make this cake every year on my birthday? No matter what presents I got or didn't get, I always knew I'd have this to enjoy. Do you remember that?" Janie nodded.

She did remember a bit about those birthday parties. She was very young at the last one though. When she thought really hard and closed her eyes tight, she could remember Mimi's laugh and the way she smelled like pink lotion.

"Well, Baby," Mother was saying, "no one else could make this cake. It was a special gift that only my mother could give me, because it belonged to her. It was something from her heart."

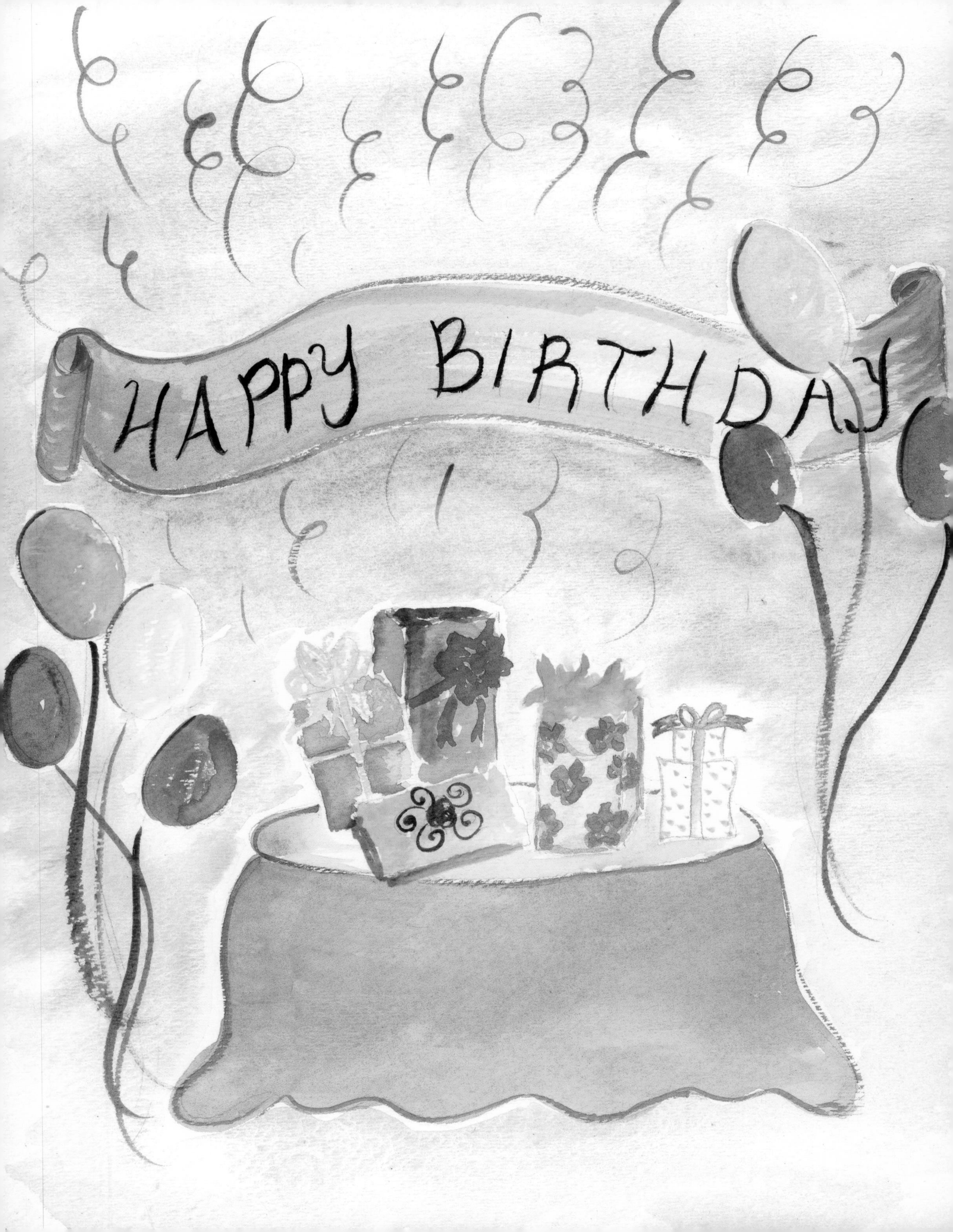
HAPPY BIRTHDAY

"So, the cake was a gift?" Janie asked.

"Yes ma'am, it wasn't just having a delicious treat. It was knowing that my mama loved me so much that she gave me something only she could. Since Mimi's passed on, I guard this gift more than gold, silver, or those fine jewels that shine through the store windows you're always looking in. And I have something special to share with my family and my friends, like she did."

"Do you mean that Mimi used to share the recipe, Mama? Then why won't you?"

"No, baby, Mimi used to share the cake, not the recipe. When I was young, she always baked something on Saturdays. Sometimes she baked during the week also, but there was always a fresh cake on Saturday. She'd be taking it to share with a friend who needed some cheering up, or to somebody who was feeling ill. I saw her take unique cakes to homes before funerals, homes with new babies and even to the voting precincts."

"Why the voting places?" Janie asked.

"Well, Mimi just seemed to know when somebody needed a sweet surprise. She also knew those people working at the polls got bored being there all day. A cake seemed to turn the election into a celebration. I heard that those folks would all sign up to work on Election Day just because they knew something delicious would be in store for them. People would ask her for the recipe and she'd tell them that she couldn't give it, but she'd be happy to make one for them."

Janie's eyes got bright. "Mama, that's what you say!"

"Well, I suppose that I heard it enough growing up that it stuck.  I do hope that a lot of other things my mother taught me have sunk in as well.  And, Janie, do you know what else?" Janie's mother asked as she kept remembering, "Mimi never made something to take to other people without baking for us, too.  If the cake to be shared was finished and we wanted some, she'd tell us to go ahead and cut a piece.  She was 'making another one anyway', she'd say.  When she did that, she let us know that she loved us more than anyone else and that we came first.  But she kept on baking for other people too.  It was one of her ways to show that she cared."

Janie asked, "So Mama, who are you making this one for?  Where will you take it?"

Her mother didn't answer.  Janie noticed her mama looking at Mimi's picture in the window.  Mother was thinking about those first desserts reserved just for family. Daddy had often asked where the newest cake would be going after he lingered in the kitchen to enjoy the heavy aroma of rich chocolate.  How often did Mama take one to friends while the children scrambled to lick the beaters?

Mother giggled as she touched a little dab of icing to the end of Janie's nose. Janie stuck her tongue way out and tried her best to lick the icing away, then finally rubbed her nose against the blue gingham dishcloth that hung beside the sink.

Janie's mama stood back and admired the just finished homemade masterpiece. She felt good about her creation. "This brings back warm memories." Janie heard her whisper.

Then Mama reached over, wrapped her arm around Janie's waist and said, "Now get down, girl and let's have a piece."

"Yay!" squealed Janie as she hopped off the counter with her mother's help. "I'll get the plates. I can't wait!"

"Me either," said her mama as she carefully placed the platter on the table and slid the knife in for the first smooth cut. "After all, it is the best chocolate cake in the whole wide world."

"You know, one day baby, I will share the recipe with you.  Today, I'm sharing the cake. It's my gift."  Janie wrapped her arms around her mama's hips and squeezed as hard as she could.

As the two sat down to savor the first bites, Mama whispered, "Maybe we should save some for the boys."  Janie's teeth were covered in crumbles of chocolate as she laughed and said, "Or we could just make another one."

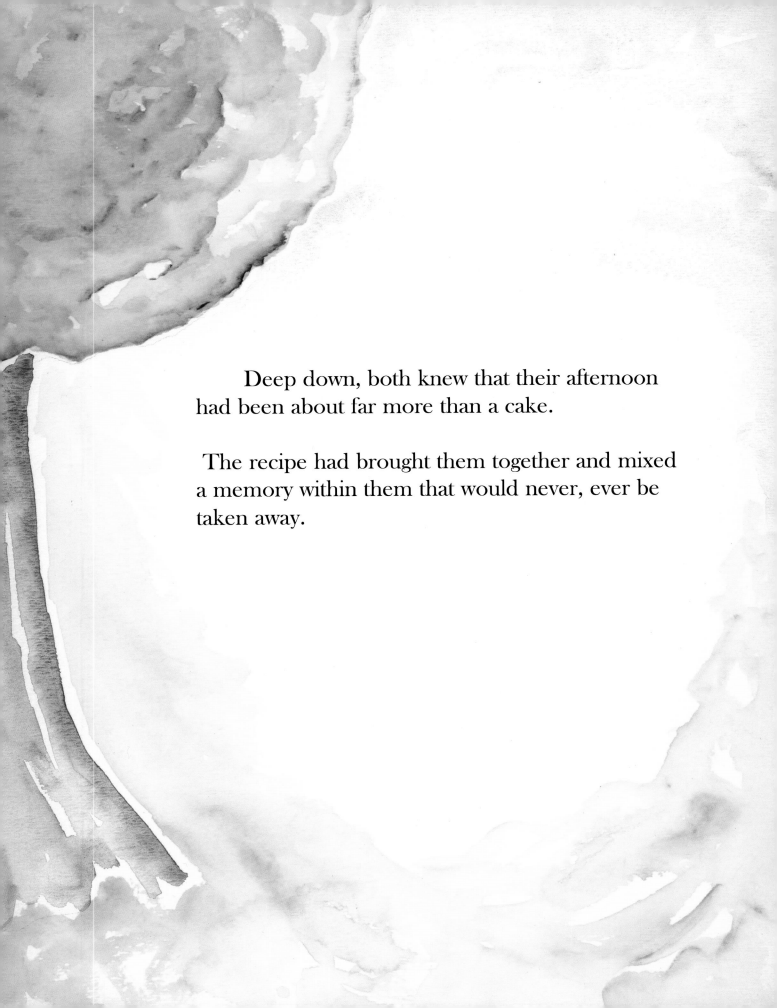

Deep down, both knew that their afternoon had been about far more than a cake.

The recipe had brought them together and mixed a memory within them that would never, ever be taken away.

Tishomingo Tree Press, 606 Bay Street, Hattiesburg Mississippi 39401
Phone: 1-601-582-0116

info@tishomingotree.com
www.tishomingotree.com